D1466695

Mushu's Story

Ron Fontes and Justine Korman

DISNEY PRESS

New York

Adapted from
Walt Disney Pictures' MULAN
Music by MATTHEW WILDER Lyrics by DAVID ZIPPEL
Original score by JERRY GOLDSMITH
Produced by PAM COATS
Directed by BARRY COOK and TONY BANCROFT

Printed in Mexico

ISBN: 0-7868-4225-3 (paperback)

chapter one

*T*his is the story of a terrible war that took place long ago. Shan-Yu, brutal leader of the Hun warriors, crossed the Great Wall into China. The emperor of China commanded that one man from every family report for army service and . . .

Wait! This is the story of *me*, Mushu! *I* saved China! Okay, I had some help from a girl named Mulan. But she caused me big trouble, as you will see.

One night, in the Fa family temple where the ancestors and guardians rest, the First Ancestor woke me. I was eager to defend the Fa family, but the First Ancestor pointed at the other statues and said, "These are the family guardians. You, Oh Demoted One . . ."

"I ring the gong," I grumbled. Make one mistake and they never let you forget it. So I

banged the gong, and the temple filled with the spirits of the Fa Ancestors.

The buzz was that Mulan had run away!

You see, the Huns, led by the evil Shan-Yu, had invaded China.

The emperor ordered one man from each family to join the Imperial Army. Mulan's father, Fa Zhou, had no sons, so he was determined to fight.

To save her father, Mulan decided to take

his place. But the laws also said a girl could not disguise herself as a boy. If Mulan got caught, Fa Zhou would be shamed forever and Mulan would lose her head! Something had to be done.

"Let a guardian bring her back," an ancestor suggested.

The ancestors wanted the most cunning and powerful guardian. Modestly, I stepped forward. "I'll go," I said.

The foolish ancestors laughed at me.

"You don't think I can do it?" I cried. "Jump back!" I puffed my cheeks and made a flame. I *am* a dragon after all. "Pretty hot, huh?"

The First Ancestor wasn't impressed. "You had your chance. You led Ancestor Fa Deng to disaster."

"Thanks a lot," said Fa Deng. This disgruntled spirit's head glared at me from under his arm. Was he still mad?

"You are unworthy of this spot," the First Ancestor said as he threw me out the door. "Awaken the Great Stone Dragon."

I banged my gong to wake old Rocky, but he didn't hear me, so I started hitting him. The mighty protector crumbled to dust!

"Have you awakened, Great Stone Dragon?" the First Ancestor called.

I looked at the rubble. I am so clever! I lifted the Stone Dragon's head above the bushes, and said in a deep voice, "Ah, yes, I am the Great Stone Dragon. I will go forth and fetch Mulan. Did I mention I was the Great Stone Dragon?"

"Go! The fate of the Fa family rests in your claws." The First Ancestor believed me!

"Don't even worry about it," I said.

Then the heavy head tipped over, and I tumbled down a hill. *Ow!*

Chirp! Chirp! A cricket hopped up. He spoke in cricket talk, but I understood him because I am so wise. He said his name was Cri-Kee.

"Why don't *you* get Mulan?" he asked.

That's when the idea hit me. If I made Mulan a hero, the ancestors would forgive

me, and make me a guardian again. I am brilliant!

I set off across the garden, and the cricket tagged along.

"What makes you think you're coming with me?" I asked him.

"I'm lucky," Cri-Kee chirped.

"You'd better be!"

chapter two

At dawn, I found Mulan in the mountains. Did I mention I am also a great tracker? She was near an army camp, practicing her "manly ways."

Mulan's "deep voice" wasn't bad. But when she drew her father's sword, Mulan fumbled and dropped the heavy blade. Her horse, Khan, laughed.

"It isn't as easy as it looks," Mulan said. "I need a miracle."

That was my cue! I lit a fire and used its light to cast a huge shadow. My voice echoed off the rocky cliffs. "Did someone ask for a miracle?"

Mulan gasped. "A ghost!"

"Get ready, Mulan," I said. "I am your guardian, the powerful, the indestructible Mushu!"

I stepped into view. "Pretty hot, huh?"

Mulan should have been impressed. Instead, it took her a while to notice me at her feet.

"My guardian is a lizard?" Mulan asked, confused.

"*Dragon!* Not lizard!" I said. "I don't do that tongue thing."

Mulan was skeptical. "But you're tiny."

"I'm travel size. If I were my real size, your cow here would die of fright." I glared at Khan.

"Well," Mulan said, "I can use all the help I can get."

"Move it, heifer!" I barked to Khan.

We had a country to save!

* * *

Soon, we arrived at the army camp. I cleverly hid inside Mulan's kerchief. "Show them your man walk," I said to her.

"Shoulders back, head up, and strut!"

"I don't think they walk like this," Mulan said uncertainly.

The smelly, dirty men scratched and spit as they gaped at her. But what did they know? I was a great coach.

"They are disgusting," Mulan muttered.

"No, they're just men," I said. "And you're going to have to act like them, so pay attention. Be tough, like this guy here." I pointed to a short, pudgy soldier.

"What are *you* looking at?" he demanded.

"Punch him," I whispered. "It's how men say 'hello.'"

In seconds, Mulan was in the center of a manly brawl with Yao and his two friends, Chien-Po and Ling. The fight spilled into the mess line. Rice rained everywhere as hungry soldiers glared at Mulan.

A stern young man stopped the fight. He was Captain Shang, the son of General Li, commander of the army.

"No one causes trouble in my camp," he barked at Mulan.

"Sorry," Mulan answered. "A guy gets those manly urges."

"What's your name?" Captain Shang demanded.

Behind the captain, Chi Fu held a writing brush poised over an ivory tablet. This self-important busybody was the emperor's counsel, a royal advisor (and a royal pain!). "Your commanding officer asked you a question!" Chi Fu said.

"I've got a . . . boy's name," Mulan said.

"Try . . . ah, Chu," I prompted.

"Ah Chu!" Mulan blurted.

"Ah Chu?" Shang repeated.

"Bless you!" I said. I laughed at my own hilarious joke.

Mulan tried to shush me. "Mushu!"

"Mushu?" Shang asked, more puzzled than ever.

"No! No!" Mulan exclaimed.

"Ping," I whispered. "Ping was my best friend growing up."

Mulan clamped her hand over my mouth. "My name is Ping," she said. "I serve in Fa Zhou's place."

Chi Fu frowned. "I didn't know the great hero had a son."

Mulan replied in her deepest voice. "He doesn't talk about me much."

Chi Fu whispered. "I can see why."

Shang addressed his troops. "Thanks to Ping, tonight you will pick up every grain of rice. Tomorrow, the real work begins!"

chapter three

The next morning, training began. Shang shot an arrow high into a tall pole. Then he brought out two heavy bronze disks.

"This disk is discipline," Shang told his troops. "The other is strength. You will need both to reach the top of the pole." The disks were tied to the wrists of each man as he climbed the pole. Each one failed!

Mulan took her turn. She pulled and strained, but the arrow was still far away.

Then, one night, Mulan got an idea.

She snatched up the disks, and tied them together. The weight of the disks helped pull her to the top.

Amazed, the soldiers cheered. Ping

had outsmarted the pole.

Too bad Chi Fu was not impressed

"Once General Li reads my report, your troops will never see battle," Mulan and I heard him say to Shang.

Shang stormed away. Boy, was he mad.

And now I had a very big problem. How could I make Mulan a hero if she didn't fight?

I decided to take matters into my own claws. First, Cri-Kee and I found a friendly panda. Then we borrowed some armor and made a fake soldier. The "soldier" gave Chi Fu urgent orders from General Li: Shang's troops must go to the front!

It worked! We were headed to battle.

chapter four

But by the time we reached the mountain village, it was too late. General Li and his troops were dead.

Shang knew there was no time for grief.

"We're the emperor's only hope," he said.

We climbed the frozen mountain. I was so cold my scales rattled. Mulan led Khan who pulled a wagon loaded with spears, bows, arrows, and rocket cannons.

But I just have to say, no one can prove that I, Mushu, made that rocket explode.

Did I mention that a rocket exploded? It was *not* my fault!

Boom! The frosty peaks echoed.

Shang galloped up to the wagon. "You just gave away our position!" he shouted at Mulan. His breath still hung in the air when *thunk!*, an arrow smacked into his armor.

Shang was knocked off his horse.

That arrow had many flaming brothers that flew down from the peaks above. They pierced the wagon, setting it ablaze.

Mulan set Khan free right before the wagon exploded. The blast knocked them to the ground. Flames shot up to the sky—and so did Cri-Kee and I!

Thump, thump. We landed in the snow just in time for Shang's counterattack. Mulan joined the soldiers behind some rocks as Shang gave the order to fire!

Cannons boomed! We could barely see through the smoke. Then all fell silent. Had we won?

The smoke cleared, and our hearts sank. We were doomed!

Shan-Yu charged down the slope, his Hun horde following him. A war falcon streaked overhead.

Shang set his jaw. "If we die, we die with honor! Yao, aim the last cannon at Shan-Yu."

Trust my Mulan to disobey an order. She pushed Yao aside, grabbed the cannon, and ran toward the Huns.

Mulan was ruining my chances to be a guardian! I hung onto her collar for dear life.

Mulan plowed through snowdrifts while the Huns headed straight for us, like an avalanche of doom. Did I say avalanche? I'm getting ahead of myself.

Shan-Yu was right in front of us.

Maybe Mulan wanted to shoot the mighty invader. I could still become a guardian!

"You might want to light that cannon now," I advised. Perhaps I sounded a little panicky. But timing *is* everything.

Mulan tried to strike a flint to light the cannon. SWOOSH! Shan-Yu's falcon swooped down and knocked the little stone from Mulan's hand.

Mulan grabbed me and pushed me against the cannon. She yanked my tail. WHOOSH! A flame shot out of my mouth and lit the fuse.

Only *I* could have lit that cannon, but I was so excited, I forgot to let go of the rocket. FOOSH! It whizzed right over Shan-Yu's head! What was going on?

"How could you miss?" I screamed back at Mulan. "He was right in front of you!"

But had she aimed the cannon at Shan-Yu? No! Mulan had pointed it at a snowy mountain peak! I let go.

KABOOM! That one little rocket started an awesome avalanche. Snow smothered Shan-Yu's army under an icy blanket. China

was saved! Three cheers for Mushu!

Shan-Yu swung his sharp sword at the smiling Mulan. She grunted in pain as Shang rushed to her side. They escaped the wall of snow. Shan-Yu didn't.

But the avalanche didn't stop. Khan galloped up to the struggling heroes. Mulan jumped on his back and reached for Shang, but it was too late. The snow swept over them.

I saw something sticking out of the whiteness. It was Cri-Kee! "Man, you are one lucky bug."

Mulan, Shang, and Khan were not so lucky. They were sliding closer to the edge of the steep cliff! I ran to Mulan. "I found the lucky cricket!"

Mulan grabbed me. "I need a rope!"

I had no rope.

Whack! An arrow with a rope attached landed right beside me. "Thanks," Mulan said, surprised. I was impressed myself that I could summon a rope from thin air. To be honest, it was tied to Yao's arrow, only he had forgotten to hold on to the other end.

But Mulan wasn't out of ideas yet. She

twisted the loose end of the rope around Khan's saddle. Then she placed the arrow in her bow and aimed high. Nice idea, but we were already falling.

Twang! Mulan's arrow headed straight for the soldiers above us. They grabbed the rope and pulled us to safety.

Shang sat up. "Ping, I owe you my life."

The soldiers cheered for Mulan. I'd done the hard part. But did they cheer for Mushu? No! Still, I was proud. Mulan was a hero!

chapter five

Suddenly, Mulan lost her smile. She touched her side. Her hand was covered with blood.

This was very bad. There was no way we could keep her secret now. While treating the wound, the doctor found out the truth.

Snooty Chi Fu dragged Mulan out of the doctor's tent.

"I knew there was something wrong with you," he shouted as he threw her on the ground. "A woman!"

The soldiers were shocked. Their hero was a mere girl!

"My name is Mulan," she said. "I did this to save my father."

"High treason! Ultimate dishonor!" Chi Fu cried.

"You know the law," he said to Shang.

So did I! The penalty for impersonating a man was death!

Shang drew Mulan's sword from her saddle. He walked toward the helpless girl.

Shang raised the deadly blade. We all held our breath. But Shang decided to do what was right, not what the law demanded. He threw down the sword. "A life for a life. My debt is repaid." He turned to his troops. "Move out."

Chi Fu protested. "But you can't just . . . "

The captain's eyes flashed. "Move out!"

The soldiers marched, and soon we were alone. I was very depressed. "I could have been on the top shelf. All my fine work . . . *pfft!*"

"I should never have left home," Mulan said sadly.

I tried to cheer her up. "You wanted to save your father's life. Who knew you would end up shaming him and your ancestors, and losing all your friends?"

Mulan sighed. "Maybe I didn't go for Father. Maybe I really wanted to prove I could do things right, so when I looked in the mirror I'd see someone worthwhile." She stared at her reflection in her helmet. "I see nothing."

Mulan blinked back tears.

"That's because it needs some spit." I

rubbed the helmet. "See? Look at you. You're so pretty."

But Mulan was not interested. "I'm sorry I wasted your time, Mushu."

I saw myself in the bright metal. I was good-looking, but was I a good guardian?

"The truth is," I confessed, "we're both frauds. The ancestors never sent me."

Cri-Kee chirped.

"You're not really lucky?" I asked him. "You lied to me?" I turned to Khan. "What are you, a sheep?"

"Let's go home," Mulan said sadly.

"Don't worry." I said. "We started together

and we'll finish together." I gave her a big Mushu hug.

Suddenly, we heard a terrible howl. We peered over the edge of the cliff. Shan-Yu was alive, along with five of his men!

Mulan jumped up and ran to Khan.

"Home is that way." I pointed in the opposite direction.

"Are we in this together or not?" Mulan asked.

"Let's go kick some Hunny-bun!" I shouted.

chapter six

M ake way for the heroes of China!" an official declared. Shang and his men marched through the gates to the Imperial City. A cheering crowd awaited them.

The troops approached the emperor's glorious palace. Fine statues decorated the roof. A great fireworks tower looked down upon the crowded streets.

Bright kites swooped and soared above the rooftops. Huge paper dragons snaked through the jostling throng. None of those dragons was as handsome as me, but they were festive.

Mulan cried out, "Shang! The Huns are alive! They're in the city!"

The captain turned in surprise.

"Why should I believe you?" Shang asked.

He *did* have a point. Mulan had pretended to be someone she wasn't. Big lies carry a big price. But Mulan was stubborn.

"You trusted Ping," she said. "Is Mulan any different?"

Shang was silent. Mulan galloped away.

A very solemn Shang climbed the steps of the emperor's palace. A paper parade dragon followed him.

BOOM BOOM BOOM! Giant drums echoed over the palace plaza. Dressed in splendid yellow robes, the emperor emerged from a tall, heavy door.

The drums stopped. A servant rang a gong.

"China will sleep safe tonight," the emperor said. "Thanks to our brave warriors, the Huns have been defeated."

The crowd's roar sounded like a huge waterfall.

Meanwhile, Mulan tried to warn all the

people that the Huns were in the city.

"They won't listen!" Mulan was frantic.

"You're just a girl," I said. "What do you expect?"

On the palace steps, Shang knelt and presented Shan-Yu's sword to the emperor.

"Your father would have been very proud," the emperor said.

Suddenly a falcon swooped down and seized the sword! The bird flew over the palace roof and dropped the sword into the hands of a rooftop statue.

What was this? It was no statue. It was Shan-Yu!

chapter seven

The crowd gasped in horror.

The paper dragon on the steps split open, and Shan-Yu's men slashed free of their hiding place. They knocked Shang down, seized the emperor, and carried him into the palace.

Shang lifted his head as the emperor's tall hat rolled down the steps.

Yao, Ling, and Chien-Po ran to help their captain save the emperor. But the palace doors were barred!

With a mighty heave, the soldiers tipped over a stone statue. They used it as a battering ram, but the doors wouldn't budge.

Mulan shook her head. "They'll never reach the emperor in time."

"Hey, guys, I have an idea." She convinced Yao, Ling, and Chien-Po to join her, but Shang hung back. He was still angry at Mulan.

Only Mulan could have come up with such a wild idea! She dressed her friends in women's finery. They painted their faces and wore fancy wigs.

Shan-Yu's men barely noticed the ugly "women" giggling behind their fans until Mulan and her friends dropped their

disguises. The startled Huns never knew what hit them.

Luckily, Shang decided to help us. So, while Mulan and the boys were taking care of the soldiers, Shang raced to where Shan-Yu was threatening the emperor.

"Your walls have fallen, and so have you. Bow to me!" Shan-Yu ordered.

The emperor said bravely, "No matter how the wind howls, a mountain cannot bow to it."

Shan-Yu brandished his huge sword. "Then you will kneel in pieces!"

chapter eight

Shang sprang and blocked the blade. He and the Hun battled to the edge of the palace tower.

Mulan pointed to a line of lanterns hanging from the tower.

"Chien-Po," she yelled, "get the emperor!"

Chien-Po lifted the ruler of all China and carried him to the ground on the rope slide. Yao and Ling followed.

Meanwhile, Shan-Yu had flattened Shang like a rag doll. With a ferocious growl, he turned to Mulan.

Mulan cut the slide before Shan-Yu could reach it. Shan-Yu peered over the side, searching for the emperor. He only saw thousands of citizens, cheering their emperor's escape. Shan-Yu put his sword to Shang's throat. He rumbled, "You took away my victory!"

Mulan' yelled at the Hun. "No, I did!" She pulled her hair back to show Shan-Yu her face.

Shan-Yu recognized the "soldier" who had defeated him in the mountains. He charged!

As she ran down a hallway Mulan grabbed me. The sound of Shan-Yu smashing everything in his path was close behind.

Mulan started to whisper something, but, clever as I am, I was way ahead of her.

"C'mon, Cri-Kee!"

We jumped onto a kite and floated over to the fireworks tower.

I said to the men in charge of the fireworks, "Citizens, I need firepower."

"Who are you?" a man asked.

I flapped the kite like big wings. "Your worst nightmare!"

The soldiers, awed by the sight of the terrible Mushu, leaped to safety.

Meanwhile, Mulan, still being chased by Shan-Yu, had crawled onto the roof of the palace. She had nowhere to go, and nothing but a fan to protect her.

Mulan opened the fan.

"Looks like you're out of ideas," Shan-Yu sneered.

He thrust his sword through the painted silk. Mulan snapped the fan shut and twisted the weapon from Shan-Yu's grip.

"Not quite," Mulan said. She pinned the Hun's tunic to the roof with his own sword. "Ready, Mushu?"

I was ready. I had a rocket strapped to my back, and a cricket ready to light it. I breathed flame on a stick and handed it to Cri-Kee. "Light me!" I exclaimed.

The fuse sizzled and . . . WHOOSH! I shot through the air straight at Shan-Yu.

Cri-Kee and I jumped free of the rocket

just before it struck the surprised Hun. Shan-Yu flew on flaming wings—straight into the fireworks tower.

Fireworks shot everywhere! BOOM! POP! POW! CRACKLE! Colorful blossoms burst into bloom, raining sparks and debris on the astonished crowd.

Once again, I, Mushu, had saved the day—with a little help from Mulan.

chapter nine

Shang and Mulan rose from the rubble.

"Where is she? Now she's done it."

Who could that shrill voice belong to? Why, Chi Fu! Scorched and singed, he screeched, "Stand aside! That creature is not worth protecting!"

He meant Mulan, of course.

"She's a hero," Shang said.

"She's a *woman*," Chi Fu countered. "Worthless!"

"Listen, you pompous—"

"That is enough," the emperor's commanding voice said.

The emperor approached Mulan. "I have

heard a great deal about you, Fa Mulan," the celestial ruler said. "You stole your father's armor and ran away from home. You impersonated a soldier, deceived your commanding officer, dishonored the Chinese Army, destroyed my palace, and . . . "

Mulan trembled like a leaf in a storm. What terrible fate did she face?

" . . . and," the emperor continued, "you have saved us all."

Mulan dared to raise her eyes to the emperor. He smiled and did the unthinkable—he bowed to Mulan!

Chi Fu was in shock. But he bowed, too. Mulan's friends, and then all the citizens, bowed to *my* Mulan. I wept with pride, knowing it was all due to my guidance.

Then the emperor appointed Mulan to his council. Of course, he had to fire Chi Fu, but no one minded.

"With all due respect, Your Excellency," Mulan said modestly, "I think I've been away from home long enough."

The emperor nodded. He took the pendant from his neck. On it was the Imperial crest. "Take this," he told her, "so your family will know what you have done for me. And take Shan-Yu's sword, so the world will know what you have done for China."

Mulan hugged the emperor.

"Is she allowed to do that?" Yao whispered.

Mulan turned to Shang. He could barely speak. He shook Mulan's hand. "Um, you're, um. You fight good," he stammered.

"Thank you." Not knowing what else to say, she mounted Khan and rode away.

The emperor cleared his throat. "The flower that blooms in adversity is the most rare and beautiful of all," he said to Shang.

"Sir?"

"You don't meet a girl like that every dynasty," the emperor said wisely.

chapter ten

Mulan presented the sword and the Crest to her father. These were a great honor. But to Fa Zhou, the greatest honor was having Mulan for a daughter.

Shang appeared, making excuses for following Mulan home. Mulan just smiled and asked him to stay for dinner.

But let's get to the most important part of the story: me! The ancestors in the family temple were so pleased, that I got to be a guardian again!

And that is the story of how I, Mushu, saved all of China, three or four times at least. There is no more to say.